P9-ARL-468

WITHDRAWN

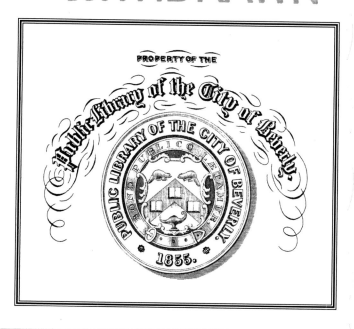

PROPERTY OF THE

Public Library of the City of Beverly.

PUBLIC LIBRARY OF THE CITY OF BEVERLY

BONO PUBLICO

1855.

MONSTER and Boy

Henry Holt and Company, *Publishers since 1866*
Henry Holt® is a registered trademark of Macmillan Publishing Group, LLC
120 Broadway, New York, NY 10271 · mackids.com

Text copyright © 2021 by Hannah Barnaby
Illustrations copyright © 2021 by Anoosha Syed
All rights reserved.

Library of Congress Control Number: 2020910180

ISBN 978-1-250-21785-1

Our books may be purchased in bulk for promotional, educational, or
business use. Please contact your local bookseller or the Macmillan
Corporate and Premium Sales Department at (800) 221-7945 ext. 5442 or
by email at MacmillanSpecialMarkets@macmillan.com.

First edition, 2021 / Designed by Mallory Grigg
Printed in the United States of America by LSC Communications,
Crawfordsville, Indiana
10 9 8 7 6 5 4 3 2 1

For all of the teachers
and librarians who make
Kids + School = magic.
—H. B.

For Zayna and Zaayan.
—A. S.

MONSTER'S FIRST
DAY OF SCHOOL

Hannah Barnaby

Illustrated by Anoosha Syed

GODWIN BOOKS

HENRY HOLT AND COMPANY
NEW YORK

YOU KNOW THAT FEELING, WHEN YOU'RE SURE YOU'VE met someone before but you just can't quite remember where it was? It's different than when you see someone you know but they just got a crazy new haircut and suddenly you can't remember what they looked like yesterday. It's also different than when you see your teacher at the grocery store and she's buying the same cereal you like.

Right now, I'm having that first feeling. Not the other two.

Haven't we met, you and I?

Don't I know you?

Maybe it's because you're holding this book and it's the second book with this monster and this boy in it. Do I know you from the first Monster and Boy book? The one where the monster swallowed the boy and then the boy was tiny and he fell in the toilet and there was another monster in the kitchen?

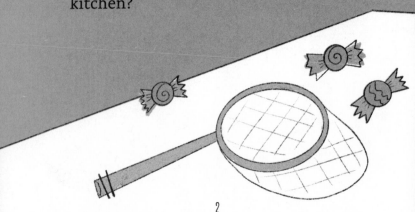

That must be it.

You just look so *familiar*.

Anyway.

If that's not where I know you from, you might want to go get the first Monster and Boy book now. I mean, this one is perfectly good to read all on its own, but if you're the kind of person who likes to do things in the proper order . . .

Well, it's really up to you.

I'm just the narrator.

1.

Once there was a monster who loved a boy. And a boy who loved a monster.

They hadn't always known each other. The monster lived under the boy's bed for a long time before they met, and the boy didn't know the monster was there until one night when the monster decided to introduce himself. And now they were friends.

Here is a list of things the boy and the monster liked to do together:

1. Use the boy's mother's fancy gels and sprays to make funny hairstyles on the boy and furstyles on the monster.

2. Draw pictures of themselves having adventures, saving the world, and wearing matching hero suits.

3. Ask questions.

That third one was really more the monster's thing.

The monster had a lot of questions.

"Why don't eyebrows grow long like the rest of your hair? Why are eggs so smooth? Why do elbows only bend one way? How fast can a duck run?"

The boy did his best to answer the monster's questions.

Luckily, the monster didn't mind at all if the boy's answer was "I don't know."

(Some people will try and tell you that "I don't know" is not a proper answer to a question. If that ever happens to you, you may inform them that curiosity is a valuable thing.)

If the boy didn't know an answer, he did his best to find it. The first place he always looked was his bookshelf. The boy had a huge bookshelf with lots and lots of books on it.

When the monster had a question about stars, the boy showed him a book about space.

When the monster had a question about teeth, the boy showed him a book about bodies.

When the monster had a question about raccoons, the boy showed the monster a book about animals.

The book said that some animals were awake at night. That was called *nocturnal*. Some animals were awake during the day. That was called *diurnal*. And some animals were awake at the beginning of the day and at the end.

"That sounds like me," said the monster.

"Then you are *crepuscular*," the boy told him.

"Ooh," said the monster. "That sounds fancy."

"And it rhymes with *muscular*," the boy pointed out.

"Am I that, too?"

The boy studied the monster for a minute. "I can't really tell," he said.

Then the monster and the boy went back to what they had been doing before, which was spying on animals through their binoculars.

(*Binoculars* was another word that the monster thought sounded fancy. And he didn't know this yet, but those binoculars were about to become very, very important.)

2.

Now that they were friends, the monster missed the boy while he was gone all day. There were many things to look at in the boy's room: toys, books, interesting clothes with interesting patterns.

But playing alone was no fun. The monster didn't know how to read. And most of the boy's clothes were much too small for the monster to wear.

The monster didn't understand why some days were different than other days, if they all ended with *day*. He especially didn't understand why, on some days, the boy stayed home and played and read books and built pillow forts and snuck cookies upstairs, but on other days, the boy woke up, got dressed, and went somewhere else.

He didn't understand it, and he definitely didn't like it.

Finally, one afternoon, he had a little bit of what you and I might call "a tantrum."

wham!

He stomped. He huffed. He kicked a wall and hurt his toe.

"What's wrong?" asked the boy.

"Nothing," said the monster.

"Usually, when I say nothing's wrong, I actually mean that everything's wrong," the boy remarked.

"Well, not _everything_ is wrong," the monster said.

"Then what?"

The monster looked at the boy, who he loved even though he was mad.

"Why do you keep leaving every day?" he asked. "I don't like it here when I'm by myself."

"I'm sorry," said the boy. "But I have to go to school."

"That sounds made up."

"It's real," the boy promised.

"What is it?"

"It's more of a *where* than a *what*. It's a big building where kids go to learn new things."

"You have to learn new things every day? Don't you know everything already?"

"Not even close."

The monster thought about all
the stuff the boy knew about that he
didn't. Which things had wheels,
what an elephant sounded
like, what to put on a sandwich
(peanut butter), what not to put
on a sandwich (Band-Aids). The
boy could build towers and stand
on one foot and read anything,
even a book he'd never read before.

The monster thought the boy was
magic.

And if school was where the
boy learned all those things,
then the monster wanted to
go there, too.

3.

There were a few small problems with the monster's plan to go to school, as you can imagine.

For one thing, the monster had never gone anywhere. Unless you count the kitchen.

Also, the monster was not—as far as

he knew—invisible. Which meant that everyone else at school would be able to see him.

Also, the monster was crepuscular. Which meant that he slept for most of the day. Which was when school was happening.

There seemed very little point in going to school if he was just going to fall asleep as soon as he got there.

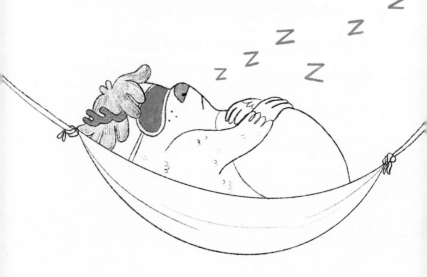

The monster needed to ask more questions.

"How do you get to school?" he asked the boy.

"I ride the bus," the boy said.

The monster didn't know this word, but it sounded a bit like *horse*, and he knew people rode on the backs of those. "How big is the bus?"

"Oh, it's huge. There's probably fifty seats in it."

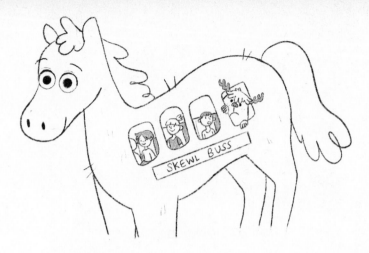

"You ride *inside* the bus?"

"Of course!"

"Ew," said the monster. But then
he remembered that the boy had been
inside of *him*, and hadn't minded too
much. Maybe the boy was just used to
being inside of things. He asked his
next question.

"Do you have to stay awake the
whole time?"

"Yes."

"Hm," said the monster. He would have to work on his endurance. "Are the other kids at school easily frightened?"

"These are strange questions," said the boy.

"Not at all," said the monster. "These are things I need to know if I'm going to come with you. I am simply trying to be prepared."

"Come *with* me?"

"Of course," said the monster.

"Oh boy," said the boy.

The monster had learned that sometimes *oh boy* meant "exciting," but sometimes it meant "uh-oh." This sounded like the "uh-oh" kind.

"I can't just take you with me. Everyone will see you."

"What if I could hide?"

"You're too big to hide."

"What if I was invisible?"

"You can make yourself invisible?"

The monster sniffed. "No."

"Maybe if you were smaller . . ."

"Hey, remember when I swallowed you and it made you tiny?"

"Yes. I don't think I'm going to forget that. Like, ever."

"Maybe it works the other way, too."

"But there's no way I can swallow you. You're way too big. And you're covered in fur. And your antlers are really pointy."

The monster and the boy sat without saying anything for what felt like a very long time but was probably only two minutes.

(Neither of them set a timer, so we can't be exactly sure.)

Then the boy said one of the monster's favorite words. "Binoculars!"

The monster was always happy to hear a word he loved, but he didn't understand why the boy was saying it now.

Binoculars made things look bigger, not smaller. And he didn't want to *look bigger*. He wanted to *get smaller*.

He also didn't want to admit that he didn't understand.

Maybe you don't understand, either.

I think I can help.

4.

Here I shall share something from the first story
about the monster and the boy, which
is a sort of monster's nursery rhyme:

Monsters have a special way of
making dreams come true.
Anything a monster dreams is what
the world must do.

When you sleep, what's all around
turns into what you see.
So close your eyes, and make the
world a bit more monsterly.

The monster learned this rhyme
from his mother, and it came in very
handy when the boy shrank to the
size of a grasshopper and he and the
monster wanted to make him big again.

things look
smaller

things look
bigger

I will also tell you something
interesting about binoculars.

If you look through the small end,
things look bigger. But if you look
through the big end, things look
smaller.

One more thing: Chances are good
that you will dream about the last
thing you see before you fall asleep.

The boy knew all these things and the monster only knew one of them. But after the boy told the monster all three, then the monster knew them, too. That's why it's important to talk about what you know instead of just keeping it all inside your head. It also gives you less stuff to have to remember. And it makes room for new stuff.

The alphabet song is the same as "Twinkle, Twinkle, Little Star"!

A cow has four stomachs!

So does a goat!

I feel so much better.

Thank you for listening.

35

36

5.

Once the boy had explained all the things to the monster that I just explained to you—well, not *all* the things, just the one about the big end of the binoculars—the monster began to understand the boy's idea much, much better. Which made him want to go to school even more, because he found that he quite liked the feeling of learning new things.

"Are you sure it will work?" the monster asked.

"I think it will. And if it doesn't, we'll think of something else."

The monster admired the boy's positive attitude. He also admired the boy's hair and how the boy kept it all on just his head instead of all over his arms and legs.

"Do the other kids at school all look like you?" the monster asked.

"Not exactly," said the boy. "Some are boys like me, and some are girls like my sister."

"Do the girls all wear monster costumes?"

"Almost never," said the boy.

"What else?" asked the monster.

"Well . . ." The boy
thought. "Some of us like
vegetables and some of
us don't. Some of us are
good at soccer and some of
us aren't. Maisy can draw
pretty much anything you
ask her to. And Ahmed
can say the alphabet
backward, and Deja can do
a handstand for like ten
minutes."

"Wow," said the
monster. "That is a lot of
information."

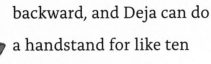

The boy shrugged. "You don't need to remember everything," he said. "I'll be there the whole time."

That made the monster feel much better.

That night, before the boy went to bed, he set up the plan.

"Lie down," he told the monster. The monster did. He wanted to show the boy that he was a good listener and very ready to go to school.

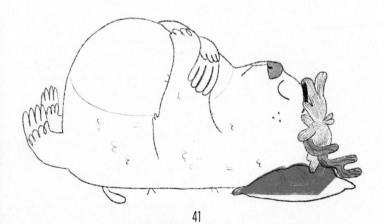

The boy made a tower out of books that reached his knee. Then he placed a small, square mirror on top of the stack of books so the monster could see himself in it. Then he handed the monster his binoculars.

"Look through the big end," said the boy, and the monster did. He saw himself in the mirror. He looked far away. He looked smaller.

But he still didn't look *small*.

"What if I don't get small enough?" he asked the boy.

The boy thought. "We might need to do this for a few nights in a row," he said, "and then you could get a little bit smaller every day until we find the right size."

The monster liked this idea. He had always just been one size. Or, he couldn't remember being any other size than the size he was now. Either way, he thought it would be fun to try out some different sizes.

What the monster didn't know is
that it can be very frustrating to be
smaller than you were before.

The monster didn't know this.

But he was about to learn.

6.

While we wait to find out whether or not the boy's plan worked, we can talk about something *you* are interested in. I've done so much talking already, and I've barely given you a turn. How terribly rude of me!

Go ahead! Anything you want!

Ah.

Mm-hm. That is fascinating.

You don't say!

Well, I am certainly glad that we had this little chat. I had no idea that you were such an interesting person.

Shall we get back to our story?

7.

When the monster woke up in the morning . . .

Wait, you're thinking, *I thought the monster was nocturnal. That's what you said in the first book. Why was he sleeping during the night?*

Well, you are correct that the monster was nocturnal when he and

the boy first met. But the monster liked spending time with the boy so much that he trained himself to sleep a little bit at night and a little bit during the day. So now, instead of being nocturnal, the monster was crepuscular.

So, being crepuscular, the monster woke up just before dawn.

When he first woke up, he completely forgot to check to see if he was a different size.

Has that ever happened to you?

You're really excited about something when you fall asleep but then you wake up and think it's just a regular morning. So you just do all your regular morning things—you blow up a balloon and pet your llama and put your bathing suit on over your clothes—and then suddenly you remember the exciting thing and it's not a regular morning anymore.

This is what happened to the monster.

But it's not what happened to the boy, who leaped out of bed and stuck his head into the underneath-the-bed and shouted, "Are you small?"

The monster was so startled that he rolled into a ball and then rolled to the farthest corner of the underneath-the-bed. And then he thought, *Oh.* Because he had always been much too big to roll around under the bed like that.

He unrolled himself.

He crept out into the boy's room.

He stood up in front of the boy.

He stared at the boy's knee, which was right in front of his face.

"It worked!" they both shouted.

A voice called from downstairs, "Are you dressed yet? You're going to be late!"

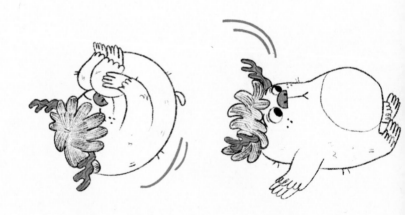

(The voice belonged to the boy's mother, who was a little cranky after discovering that she was mysteriously out of fancy hair gels and sprays.)

"Coming!" the boy called back, and then he looked at the monster.

"You're still kind of big," he said.

The monster looked down at himself. He looked up at the boy. "I don't feel very big," he said.

"Let's see if you fit in my backpack,"
said the boy.

He tucked his hands under the
monster's arms to pick him up. That
was when they learned something new.

The monster was very, very ticklish.

honk!

HONK HONK!

HONK

he he he
he he!

The monster made a loud
noise that was like a laugh
mixed with the sound of a
car alarm.

"What are you doing up
there?" the boy's mother
called. "You do not have
time for whatever it is!"

"Nothing!" called the
boy. Then he said to the
monster, "How about I hold
the backpack open and you
get in it yourself?"

ha-ha!

HA
HA HA
HA HA

HON

honk!

HAHA

HA H
HA!

HA!

honk!

HONK!

HONK
HONK

HAW
HAW!

HONK!

This worked much better, and the monster fit in the backpack quite well (once he had tucked all his fur in so it didn't get stuck in the zipper). The boy hoisted the backpack up onto his shoulders with a grunt.

"You're still kind of heavy, too," he said.

huff!

The monster tried to make himself lighter by thinking about feathers. "Did that help?" he called.

"I don't know what you mean," the boy replied, "and *please* try to remember not to talk."

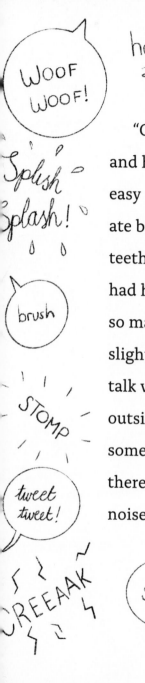

"Okay," said the monster, and he meant it. And it was easy to not talk while the boy ate breakfast and brushed his teeth because the monster had heard all those noises so many times. But it was slightly more difficult to not talk when the boy walked outside because there were some new noises, and then there was a very new, very big noise and that was the bus.

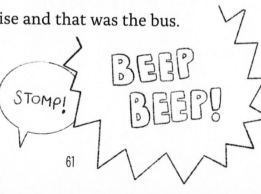

Okay, the monster told himself, *you are inside a bus. Try not to panic.*

This was very important because when monsters panic, they get sweaty. And monster sweat is a very powerful smell. It's a smell that is difficult to describe, but it's a little bit like a swamp full of maple syrup. Or a basement full of cotton candy. And if the boy's backpack started smelling like swamp syrup, everyone would know the monster was in there. Or that *something* was in there.

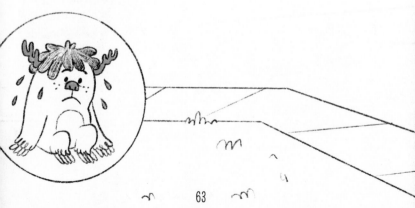

One way the monster kept himself from panicking was by singing to himself.

The boy had told him to not talk, but he hadn't said anything about not singing.

And the bus was so loud, surely no one would hear him.

Right?

As quietly as he could, the monster started singing his favorite song.

"*I wear my bathrobe in the baaaaaath—*"

The bus was suddenly much less loud.

"What was that?" the monster heard a girl's voice ask.

"That?" he heard the boy say. "That was . . . me. I was . . . singing."

"About a bathrobe?" the girl asked.

". . . Yes," said the boy.

The next sound the monster heard was a *VVVVVVVPT!* It was the zipper on the boy's backpack, which was filled

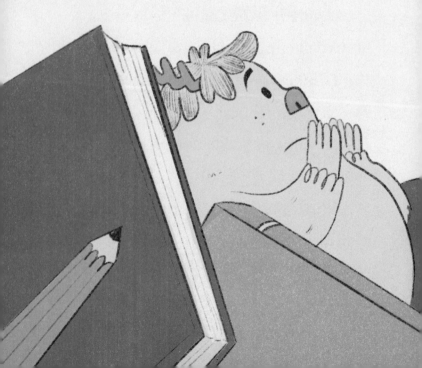

Shhh!

with sunlight and then the boy's face.

"No singing, either," he pleaded.

"Sorry," said the monster, and usually when he said *sorry* the boy said *it's okay*. But this time he didn't have a chance, because they had arrived.

8.

I will tell you right away that school was not at all what the monster expected.

For one thing, the building was absolutely enormous and the students all looked like giants and the teachers looked even bigger. (You and I both know that this is because the monster was so much smaller than usual, and when you are small, lots of things and places and people look terrifically large. When you are very small, the whole world is pretty much just like a forest of grown-ups' legs.)

School was noisy in a way that the boy's house was not. Even when the boy and his sister were yelling like pirates and sword-fighting and watching loud movies, the house was not loud like this.

It got a little bit better when the monster tucked himself deeper into the boy's backpack. It was nice and dark in there, and the boy's sweatshirt—which he had taken off at the bus stop, even

though his mother told him to wear
it—was like a very cozy blanket for
the monster to snuggle into, and the
monster's eyes started to droop . . .

No! the monster thought. I must not
fall asleep! I am at school!

Suddenly, a girl's voice said, "What's that?"

"It's, uh, a stuffed animal," said the boy. "My grandmother got it for me."

The monster didn't know what a stuffed animal was. He didn't know whether stuffed animals should speak or not. He took a chance.

"I'm crepuscular!" he announced.

The girl looked very surprised. But she didn't run away.

"Is that for show-and-tell?" she asked the boy.

". . . Yes." The boy was using his *not very sure of things* voice. The monster recognized that voice.

"Cool," said the girl, and she walked to another part of the room.

"No talking!" the boy whispered into the backpack.

The monster didn't answer.

"Did you hear me?" the boy whispered.

"Yes," whispered the monster, "but you told me not to talk."

"Maybe this wasn't a good idea," said the boy.

"I can do not talking," said the monster. "Watch."

The monster pressed his lips together—gently, because his teeth were sharp—and looked up at the boy with what he hoped was a sweet expression on his face.

"Okay," said the boy. "I have to go to my desk now. I'll come check on you in a little while."

The monster did not like the idea of the boy leaving him alone in the cubby, but he did not want to break any rules so soon after arriving at school. Rules were a big thing at school. The boy had made that very clear. Several times.

At least the cubbies were open
to the room, so the monster could
observe.

The first thing he observed was that
the boy's classroom had a lot of stuff
in it. Even more stuff than the boy's
room had. This was a relief, because
the monster was very tired of looking
at the same stuff all day. Some of the

school things were the same as what
the boy had: books, shelves, books on
shelves, a rug, posters on the walls.
But there were no toys here, or piles
of clothes, and there were many more
chairs and tables and lights.

Then the monster noticed something.

The classroom had no windows.

How did the boy know what was happening outside if there were no windows?

What if it started raining and nobody knew about it?

What if there was a terrible storm?

What if, the monster thought—and he was really letting his imagination run wild now—what if everything outside disappeared while they were in here?

The monster had frightened himself.

He whimpered.

"What was that?" a girl asked.

"Uh," said the boy.

Just then, the boy's teacher arrived.

Like so many other things, she was
not what the monster had expected.

teacher

The monster had never met a teacher before, so it is unclear what he *was* expecting, even to himself. But what he saw was a very tall woman with wild red hair that curled out in all directions. She was smiling as she came in, and her teeth were very white and looked extremely strong.

She looks just like my mother! thought the monster.

And she did. Except that she had wheels on her feet.

The boy's teacher zipped into the room on her wheels and promptly crashed into the side of her desk. All the children—including the boy— gasped.

84

"Good morning!" said the teacher.
"Did you have a good weekend? I did! I
got new roller skates!"

Slip!

Slide!

Roller skates, thought the monster. *Another beautiful word.*

He thought it would be even more beautiful out loud.

"Roller skates," he whispered.

"What was that?" asked the same girl as before.

"Uh," said the boy again.

No more out loud words, the monster told himself.

And then, being crepuscular, the monster fell asleep.

9.

When the monster woke up, something strange
was happening.

All the children—including the
boy—were sitting in a circle. They
seemed to be holding some kind of
ceremony.

The monster knew about

ceremonies because when he was a pup
(that's the word for a baby monster)
his family had held a ceremony for the
most important holiday to monsters.

I bet you think that's Halloween,
don't you?

I'm sorry, but that is incorrect.

The most important holiday to
monsters is Arbor Day.

Why? Well, because most monsters spend a great deal of time under beds, and most beds are made of wood, and Arbor Day is all about trees. Also, almost no one else of any species does anything to celebrate Arbor Day, so the monsters pretty much have it all to themselves.

They like that.

a book about rockets

tarantula

Succulent

Monsters are not naturally good at sharing.

"Okay, everyone," the teacher said. "If you brought something for show-and-tell today, you may quietly go get it and quietly return to the sharing circle."

Eeeeeeep, the monster thought excitedly, and he was very proud of

definitely a
stuffed
animal

himself for keeping that sound inside
of himself. He held perfectly still as
the boy lifted him out of the backpack,
and he was proud of himself for that,
too. He did his very best not to wiggle
as the boy carried him to the circle and
set him down on the rug.

This is going to be great, thought the
monster.

It turned out that the girl who had heard the monster whisper *roller skates* and had also heard the monster whimper had a name. Her name was Lila Durbin. The monster thought this was a lovely name, and he was very tempted to whisper it out loud, but he stopped himself.

It also turned out that Lila Durbin— like the boy—had brought something special for show-and-tell. But before I tell you what it was, I shall tell you something important about monsters.

Monsters love anything that looks like fur. Grass, shag carpet, very messy hair, pine trees, pom-poms, hedgehogs. And when monsters love something, they sometimes have a little trouble with self-control. (You may recall that our monster and our boy had quite an adventure after a swallowing-a-friend incident.)

Unfortunately for the monster, for show-and-tell that day, Lila Durbin had brought something furry-looking.

It was not a pine tree.

It was not a shag carpet.

It was Spike. Her hedgehog.

hedgehog

"Oh my gosh," whispered the monster.

"What?" whispered the boy.

"I need to hug that," whispered the monster.

"Please don't," whispered the boy.

"I have to!"

"No, you don't!"

Another girl sitting next to the boy looked over. "Are you talking to your stuffed animal?" She smiled. "I do that sometimes, too."

The teacher tapped the girl on the shoulder. "Maisy," she said. "Let's listen to Lila, please."

Maisy listened. The boy listened. The monster listened.

"This is Spike," said Lila. "He's two years old. His favorite food is apples."

The monster started to wiggle a little bit. He had now learned that sitting still in sharing circle was difficult when there was a hedgehog in the room.

"Stop wiggling," the boy whispered.

"It's so fuzzy," moaned the monster.

"What *kind* of stuffed animal is that?" Maisy asked.

The teacher tapped Maisy on the shoulder again. This time, she tapped the boy on the shoulder, too. "I hope I don't have to come over here again," she said.

Maisy, the boy, and the monster hoped that, too.

"Want to see Spike run around?" Lila asked. She set Spike gently in the middle of the sharing circle.

The monster's wiggling got worse. He had now learned that sitting still in sharing circle is *impossible* when there was a hedgehog in the center of it.

The boy tried to stop the monster from wiggling. And in the process, he forgot something that *he* had learned that morning, which was that the monster was very, very ticklish.

The monster shrieked.

oops!

Maisy jumped.

Lila Durbin dove into the circle to protect Spike.

The boy changed color.

He turned extremely pink.

Show-and-tell was over.

Ruined.

Quietly, the boy and the girl and Lila Durbin and the other children left the sharing circle to put their things away. Lila put Spike back into his cage, which—just for today, the teacher had reminded everyone—was being kept in the classroom. The boy put the monster back into his backpack.

"Next is lunch," the boy told the monster. "Then gym, then math, and then we go home."

"Okay," said the monster. He felt as if he should say something else, but he didn't know what. And the boy walked away before he could think of anything.

Being crepuscular, the monster fell asleep again.

While he was sleeping, lunch happened.

Then gym happened.

The monster woke up when the boy and his class came back for math. He still had the feeling of wanting to say something. He still didn't know what to say.

Suddenly, there was a scream!

AARGHHH!

10.

Don't you hate it when you're reading a book and something really exciting happens and then the chapter ends immediately?

It's so . . .

Oh.

Sorry.

106

11.

Suddenly there was a scream!

The monster looked around. Had someone seen him? Had he scared someone even though he wasn't big anymore?

The scream was from Lila.

"Lila, what's wrong?" asked the teacher.

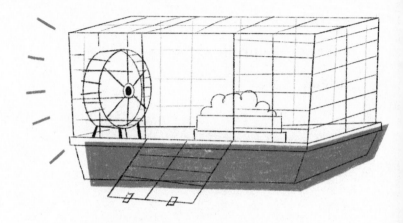

"Spike is gone!" Lila cried.

The boy looked at the monster.

The monster looked at the boy.

The boy looked at the monster.

The monster whispered, "What?"

"Did you take the hedgehog?"

"No," said the monster. "I was sleeping."

The boy's eyebrows squinched together. "Did you *take* the *hedgehog*?"

"That's the same question," said the monster helpfully. "You asked me that already."

"I want to believe you," said the boy.

"Oh, you sound just like your mother!" exclaimed the monster. "That's exactly what she said when you told her you didn't know how your baseball broke the garage window."

"Yep," said the boy.

"But . . . you *did* know how your baseball broke the garage window."

"Yep," said the boy.

"But I *didn't* take the hedgehog," said the monster.

The boy really did want to believe the monster. But nothing had ever gotten lost after show-and-tell before. And he had never brought the monster to show-and-tell before.

And Spike was fuzzy. And the monster loved fuzzy things.

The boy had a feeling in his heart.

It was not a good feeling.

He didn't know what to call it, but I do.

The feeling was doubt.

He doubted whether he could trust the monster. He doubted whether it had been a good idea to bring the monster to school, or to make him smaller, or—and this was the worst doubt of all—to become such good friends at all.

The boy wanted to hide.

Fortunately, the monster had been hiding all day already, so he had something else in mind.

"I think I can help," said the monster. He ducked into the boy's backpack.

When he reappeared, he was
holding something.

It was not a hedgehog.

It was the binoculars.

"I can help look for Spike with
these," the monster said. "I am very
good at finding fuzzy-looking things
because I love them so much."

The boy still felt doubtful, but he felt a tiny bit hopeful, too. "Okay," he said. "Let's try it."

The teacher and Maisy and Lila Durbin were all so busy looking for Spike that no one noticed the boy carrying the monster to his desk. No one noticed the monster holding the binoculars to his eyes (looking through the small end, not the big one). And no one noticed when the monster pointed to the teacher's roller skates, which were parked near the door. One of them was moving.

"Roller skates," whispered the monster.

The boy carefully scooped Spike out of the roller skate and carried him over to Lila Durbin.

Everyone cheered.

This time, when the boy turned pink, it was just a little bit. And he was smiling.

He carried the monster back to his cubby and tucked him into the backpack with the binoculars. "I didn't know you brought those," said the boy.

The monster hugged the binoculars. "I thought I might need to get big again," he said. "If something went wrong." Then he smiled. "And something did go wrong! But I fixed it without being big!"

The boy smiled, too. "I guess you did," he said. "Maybe being small isn't so bad. For now."

The monster had a feeling in his heart.

It was a very good feeling.

He didn't know what to call it, but I do.

The feeling was joy.

12.

"No wonder you are so happy to come home every day," the monster said that night. "School is noisy. School is exhausting. School is—"

"You didn't like it?" the boy asked.

The monster thought. "I *loved* it!" he said. "Can I go with you again tomorrow?"

The boy shook his head. "We only have show-and-tell once a week," he said.

"Oh," said the monster. Then he remembered something he had wanted to do at school. He whispered, "Lila Durbin."

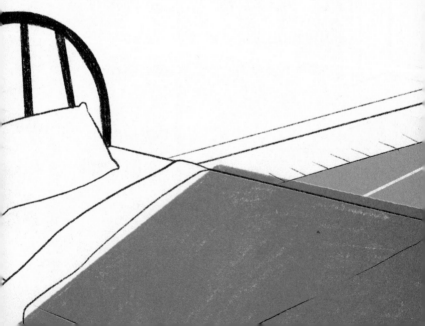

"What?" said the boy.

"Nothing," said the monster.

"Are you ready for bed?" asked the boy.

"Yes," said the monster.

"Do you have the binoculars?"

"Yes," said the monster.

"Good," said the boy. "Remember, look through the small end this time so you get big."

The monster looked at the binoculars. He thought about the day he had just spent riding around in the boy's backpack. He thought about how everything in the world looked so much bigger, and how that was scary at first but now he was used to it. He thought about how it felt to sit in the pocket of the boy's folded legs.

The monster looked at the boy.

"I think," he said, "that maybe I will stay small for a little while."

"Really?" the boy said. "I hate being small. I can't wait to be big."

"Well," said the monster, "I've been big for a long time. And I've only been small for one day."

"That makes sense," said the boy.

"The only thing is . . ." said the monster.

"What?" asked the boy.

"It feels so much bigger under the bed now that I'm small."

"Oh," said the boy.

"Do you want to sleep up here? With me?"

The monster did.

When they were both tucked in (again), the monster said, "It's too bad we don't have names like Lila Durbin."

"I have a name," said the boy.

"You do?"

"Of course," said the boy. "It's J—"

"Maybe I have a name, too, then!" the monster interrupted. "Does everyone have a name?"

"I think so," said the boy.

"Where do they come from?"

"I got mine from my mother," said the boy. "Except my father says it was his idea."

"What about your sister?" asked the monster.

"Her first name came from my grandmother, and her middle name—"

The monster interrupted again. "Your sister's middle has its own name?!" There was still so much he hadn't learned yet. It was really astonishing.

The boy yawned. "Can we talk about this tomorrow?" he asked.

The monster yawned, too. "Okay," he said.

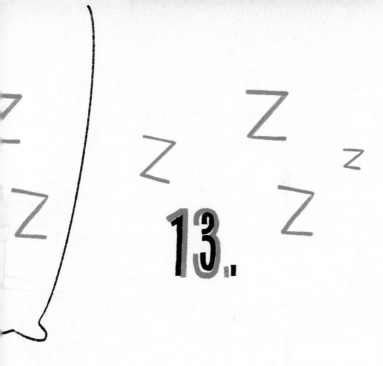

13.

The monster meant it when he said "okay," about
not talking about names until the next
day. But even though he said it and
even though he meant it, the monster
could not stop thinking about names.
He lay there, listening to the boy's
gentle breathing. He relaxed his body.

He relaxed his fur. He relaxed his antlers.

But he could not relax his mind.

Has that ever happened to you? It's very frustrating, isn't it?

To pass the time, the monster decided to make a list of names in his head. He started with *A* because, having recently learned the alphabet, it seemed like a good place to start.

A is for . . .

Right away, the monster ran into a problem. The problem was that he didn't actually *know* very many names. He especially didn't know twenty-six names, or anything that started with *Q* or *X*. (Those are always the trickiest ones in lists.)

Then the monster remembered
something. He remembered how,
when the boy said *I have a name,* he had
pointed to a painting on the wall of his
room.

The monster climbed out of the
boy's bed very carefully and quietly,
and he shuffled on his foot pads until
he could see the painting. It was a
smallish rectangle in a wooden frame.

It had five letters and each letter had a little picture next to it. There was a *J* and a jar of jelly. An *A* and an apple. An *M* and a monkey. An *E* and an egg. An *S* and a sock.

"Jelly Apple Monkey Egg Sock," said the monster. "What a beautiful name."

He sighed happily and shuffled back over to the bed. He climbed up and nestled himself next to the boy.

Maybe tomorrow, the monster thought, *I'll find my own beautiful name.*

And he fell asleep that way, and dreamed of hedgehogs on roller skates.

The End

14.

Oh no!

Granny Waffleton told me to never, ever end a book on an odd-numbered chapter!

Oh, dear. What else can I tell you?

Here are three things that you almost definitely didn't know:

1. Your sneezes leave your face at one hundred miles per hour.

2. Some snails take naps that last for three years.

3. *Genuphobia* is the fear of knees. (It is also much, much, much easier to pronounce than *Hippopotomonstrosesquipedaliophobia*. That is the fear of long words.)

Okay, that should take care of it. Now you can go have a snack.

But watch out for roller-skating hedgehogs! You know what monster dreams can do . . .